MR. BADGER AND MRS. FOX #5

THE CARNIVAL

Brigitte LUCIANI & Eve THARLET

Graphic Universe™ • Minneapolis

To my daughters ...
—B.L.

To my boys ...
—E.T.

Story by Brigitte Luciani
Art by Eve Tharlet
Translation by Carol Klio Burrell

First American edition published in 2014 by Graphic Universe™.
Published by arrangement with MEDIATOON LICENSING - France.

Monsieur Blaireau et Madame Renarde
5/Le Carnaval
© DARGAUD 2012 - Tharlet & Luciani
www.dargaud.com

Graphic Universe™
A division of Lerner Publishing Group, Inc.
241 First Avenue North
Minneapolis, MN 55401 USA

For reading levels and more information, look up this title at www.lernerbooks.com.

Library of Congress Cataloging-in-Publication Data

Luciani, Brigitte.
[Carnaval. English]
The carnival / by Brigitte Luciani ; illustrated by Eve Tharlet ;
translation by Carol Klio Burrell. — First American edition.
    p.   cm. — (Mr. Badger and Mrs. Fox ; #5)
Summary: After a long, cold winter, the foxes and badgers decide to
put on a carnival to chase away their grumpiness.
ISBN 978-1-4677-4203-0 (lib. bdg. : alk. paper)
ISBN 978-1-4677-4205-4 (eBook)
1. Graphic novels. [1. Graphic novels. 2. Carnivals—Fiction. 3. Stepfamilies—Fiction.
4. Grandparents—Fiction. 5. Badgers—Fiction. 6. Foxes—Fiction.]
I. Tharlet, Eve, illustrator. II. Burrell, Carol Klio, translator. III. Title.
PZ7.7.L83Car 2014
741.5—dc23   2013040909

Manufactured in the United States of America
1 - CG - 7/15/14

6

17

22

28